Leap Back Home to Me

LAUREN THOMPSON

illustrated by
MATTHEW CORDELL

SCHOLASTIC INC.
New York Toronto London Auckland
Sydney Mexico City New Delhi Hong Kong

Leap frog over the ladybug.

Leap frog over the bee.

Leap frog over the tickly clover,

then leap back home to me!

Leap frog over the daisies.

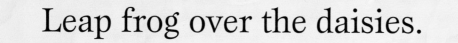

Leap frog over the creek.

Leap frog over the splashing beavers,

then leap back home to me!

Leap frog over the owl's nest.
Leap frog over the trees.

Leap frog over the rocky hilltop,

EEE!

then leap back home to me!

Leap frog over the mountains.

Leap frog over the sea.

Leap frog over the roaming clouds,

then leap frog back to me!

Leap frog over the sun.

Leap frog as high as you please.

Leap frog out to the farthest stars . . .

. . . when you leap home, here I'll be.

For Kevin
—L. T.

For Julie and Romy
—M. C.

ISBN 978-0-545-45216-8

Text copyright © 2011 by Lauren Thompson. Illustrations copyright © 2011 by Matthew Cordell. All rights reserved.
Published by Scholastic Inc., 557 Broadway, New York, NY 10012, by arrangement with Margaret K. McElderry Books,
an imprint of Simon & Schuster Children's Publishing Division. SCHOLASTIC and associated logos are trademarks
and/or registered trademarks of Scholastic Inc.

12 11 10 9 8 7 6 5 4 3 2 1   12 13 14 15 16 17/0

Printed in the U.S.A.   08

First Scholastic printing, January 2012

Book design by Lauren Rille
The text for this book is set in ITC Esprit.
The illustrations for this book are rendered
in pen and ink with watercolor.